PHILADELPHIA INTERMEDIATE UNIT NO. 26
INNOVATIVE EDUCATION PROGRAM STRATEGIES
TITLE VI IASA OF ~~1994~~ 2000 - '01

ST. ROSE OF LIMA SCHOOL

Molly and the Prince

by

MARY POPE OSBORNE

illustrated by

ELIZABETH SAYLES

An Apple Soup Book

An Imprint of Alfred A. Knopf • New York

10337

To the memory of Teddy, the dog who changed my life
—M. P. O.

To Edward Hopper and the Goatman
—E. S.

Library of Congress Cataloging-in-Publication Data

Osborne, Mary Pope
Molly and the prince / by Mary Pope Osborne : illustrated by Elizabeth Sayles.
p. cm.
An Apple Soup Book
Summary: Deep in the woods a young girl has a dream-like adventure in which she meets a goat-man and a prince who has been turned into a dog.
ISBN 0-679-81941-X (trade) — ISBN 0-679-91941-4 (lib. bdg.)
[1. Magic—Fiction. 2. Princes—Fiction.] I. Sayles, Elizabeth, ill. II. Title.
PZ7.081167Mo1   1994
[E]—dc20   93-25305

Book design by Ann Bobco

Manufactured in the United States of America
10 9 8 7 6 5 4 3 2 1

I find a dog
by the river in the reeds.
An old red dog with tattered ears.

He sniffs my hands and licks my face.
I kiss his fur, his velvet fur—
it smells like leaves.

In the bright, calm noon, he stares at me—
his eyes are deep…

I follow him down the river,

into the woods.

We chase a squirrel up a tree,

play *catch-the-stick,*

and *hide-and-seek.*

He leads me far
into the mist,
where suddenly it's hard to see.

We move like ghosts
between the trees

until he halts and sniffs the air.
The woods are still.

A shadow trembles and takes shape—
shaggy hooves,
a rough, kind face…

I start to run.

But the goat-man steps in front of me,

and deer and mice and snow-white owls
all gather near
to hear him speak.

He stares at us
and whispers in an ancient voice,
"This hound is other than he seems."
"He is?" I breathe.

He nods at me.
"This hound's a prince.
A wizard cast a wicked spell
until a girl would love him well."

"Oh!" I whisper, "Oh, I do."

Then all the forest swells with joy.
"The hound's a prince!"
And flowers fall upon us both—
    summer prince and summer girl.

The goat-man leads a long parade—
  the prince and me, deer, owls, and mice

through woods by day

and fields by night

until the moon is round and full.
He says, "Now dance!"

And while we dance, phantoms creep across the hills.

The goat-man pipes all through the night—
cries, *"Crack the whip!"*
And *"All fall down!"*

Together we roll on the ground
and laugh beneath the round, fat moon.

"Molly, dinner! Come home now,"
my brother, William, calls to me.
He's five years old.

ST. ROSE OF LIMA SCHOOL

I turn to him. The sky is gray;
the air is chilled.
"You found a dog."
"Yes, I know."

We head for home: William, me, the old stray dog.

"Whoever you think he is, he's not,"
I whisper to my brother as we eat.
 "I know," he says. "I saw his crown."

The summer hound stares up at me.
His eyes are deep,
and when they close, I know
he dreams

of the girl he found one summer's day.